A day 🔩 with the Animal Mechanics

COUGH1

KU-134-830

BRISTOL CITY COUNCIL
LIBRARY SERVICES
WITHDRAWN AND OFFERED FOR SALE
SOLD AS SEEN

ALISON
Bristol Libraries

1805362170

Sharon Rent

Dylan is helping his dad
out at work today.

This is Dad's garage. It's called Basset and Son.

Dylan likes the "and Son" bit, because that means him. It means that one day, all this will be his.

The mechanics are soon hard at work, fixing
a super-dooper-swanky-expensive posh car.
It belongs to Mr Cat the Bank Manager,
and he wants it back this afternoon
without a scratch on it.

Everyone signs in at the start of each day.

SIGN-IN SHEET

and son!

Mr Basset

Tyson the Bison

Dec the Anteater

Olivia the Ostrich

Nancy Squirrel

Car paint
is really sticky.

CAR PAINT

CAR PAINT

CAR PAINT

At work, Dad isn't called "Dad". He's called "Mr Basset",
but Dylan can't call him that because it sounds too funny.

Mechanics can fix anything with wheels.

This lorry has a flat tyre.

This car's alarm won't stop beeping.

And this bus has got chickens under
the bonnet. They didn't mean any harm.
It was just nice and warm under there.

CLUCK!

CLUCK!

Mechanics can't repair
space rockets, even
if you ask nicely.

Mechanics often look Underneath
to see what's wrong.

Big mechanics
are good at looking
under small cars,

and small mechanics are good
at looking under big cars.

These are some of the tools that mechanics use to fix things:

Pliers

Nuts
and
Bolts

Oil Can

Spanner

Wrench

Spare Tyre

Service
with a Smile

There's no point looking under this car, because it's a Total Write-Off, which means you might as well throw it in the bin.

There are lots of ways to fix things. Tyson the Bison reckons that the best way is to hit them with a spanner.

Some of the garage's customers have had an Accident.

This elephant accidentally sat on his car instead of in it.

And this dog had a crash because he accidentally put his pants on over his head. He'll need a new front bumper and grille.

A good mechanic should always check that the seats are really Bouncy. Dylan reckons these ones are fine.

Most customers are very happy with the mechanics' work.

Mrs Haddock is very glad to have her water levels topped up.

Giraffe asked them to customise his car, which means making special changes to it.

He says that his new roof and paint job are Top Notch, which means they're really, really good.

But some customers get very cross.

Apparently Mr Cat didn't want painty paw prints all over his car. Mr Daddy Basset says he can't think how they got there.

He gets his Top Mechanic to clean them off and the customer is soon happy again. Sort of.

Dylan reckons he'll soon be an Expert Mechanic.
Today he's learning that it's a good idea to close a car's
roof and windows before you press the button on the car wash.

He's also learning that tyres make a great place
to hide when the boss is angry.

Sometimes the garage is quiet.
The mechanics can tidy up and relax.

Tyson likes organising
his spanners.

Nancy relaxes
with a good stretch.

But sometimes it can be
too quiet, especially
when it's Hot.

There hasn't been a single customer all afternoon.
Where is everyone?

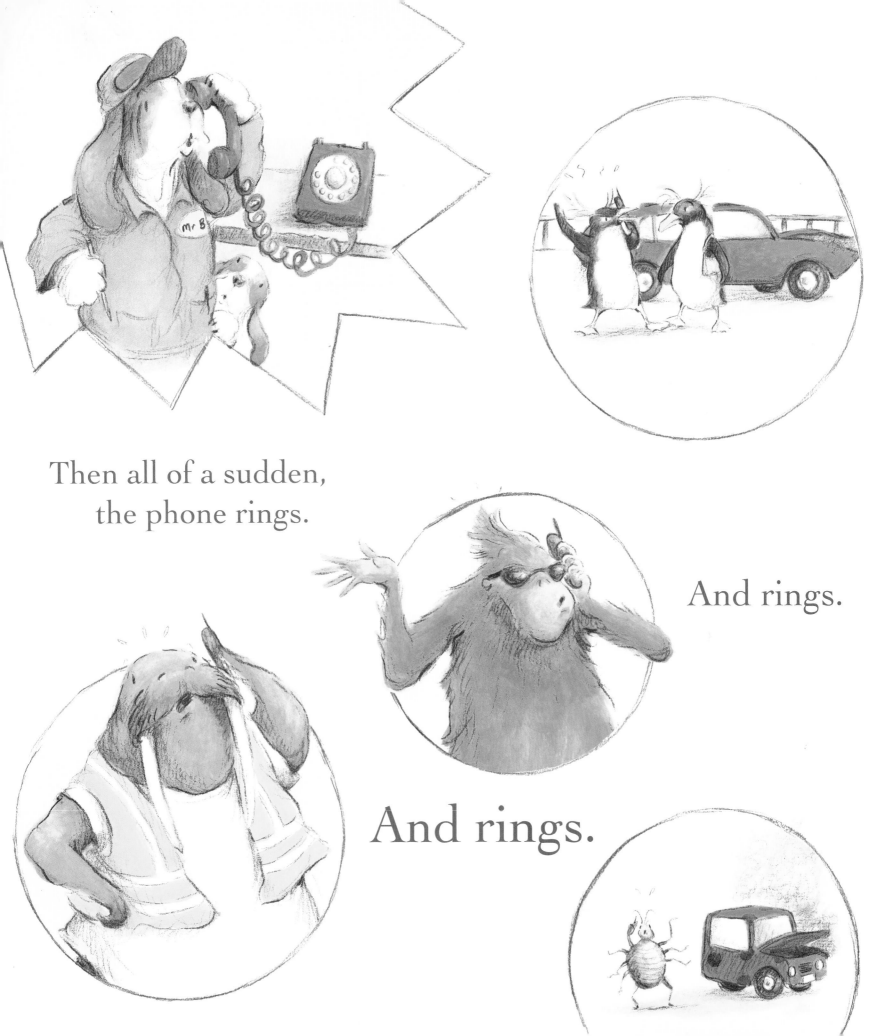

Then all of a sudden,
the phone rings.

And rings.

And rings.

Lots of cars have broken down.

Strangely, they all seem to be stuck in the same traffic jam.

It's time for the Animal Mechanics to hit the road!

Tyson

Olivia fetches some spare tyres.

Dec packs
a little snack.

Tyson grabs his
spanners, and they're
Ready for Action!

They soon see why it was so quiet at the garage.
It's such a hot day, everyone's off to the seaside.

But there's been an accident up ahead.
A load of boxes have fallen out of the back
of a lorry, and now there's an Almighty Traffic Jam.

Everyone is grumpy,
and their cars are overheating.

The mechanics quickly
set to work.

They fix tyres,

and top all the cars up
with water.

They paint over any scratches and scrapes,

and tighten all the nuts and bolts.

Dec checks everyone's oil levels.

There's a lot to do, and some of the drivers get Impatient.
Tyson has to separate some angry penguins.

Mr Daddy Basset fixes the lorry doors so they don't fall open again. Dylan has a Very Important Job: he has to pick up all the boxes.

But there's something funny about these boxes. They all feel really cold. Dylan decides to check what's in them.

It's ice cream!

Boxes and boxes of ice cream!
While the mechanics finish fixing the cars,
Dylan hands out every single one.

These are the sorts of ice cream Dylan finds:

Chocolate Lolly

Twisty Lolly

Wafer Sandwich

Rocket Lolly

Ice-Cream Cornet

Ninety-Nine

That soon gets everyone smiling
(except for the lorry driver.)
They all agree that Dylan is
the best mechanic of the lot.

At last all the vehicles are fixed,
and everyone sets off to . . .

. . . the seaside!

Good work, Animal Mechanics.
It's time for a well-earned break.

First published in 2014 by Alison Green Books
An imprint of Scholastic Children's Books
Euston House, 24 Eversholt Street, London NW1 1DB
A division of Scholastic Ltd
www.scholastic.co.uk
London ~ New York ~ Toronto ~ Sydney ~ Auckland
Mexico City ~ New Delhi ~ Hong Kong

Copyright © 2014 Sharon Rentta

HB ISBN: 978 1 407139 07 4
PB ISBN: 978 1 407139 08 1

All rights reserved
Printed in Singapore

9 8 7 6 5 4 3 2 1

The moral rights of Sharon Rentta have been asserted.

Papers used by Scholastic Children's Books
are made from wood grown in sustainable forests.

For Dala,
who's really good at fixing things.